PRAISE FOR *YOU, FROM BELOW*:

"Em J Parsley has penned *The Wizard of Oz* for modern-day Appalachia. *You, From Below* swept me into a whirlwind, and I loved every twist and turn. Parsley expertly spins the surreal into the all-too-real, delivering powerful instruction about how to push on after life as you know it has quite literally crumbled before your eyes. This book is a terror, a beauty, a comfort; it is one to hold close in hard times, for all times."

—Kristen Gentry, author of *Mama Said*

"Weaves Appalachian landscape and lore with magical realism, guiding readers on an urgent journey up a treacherous mountain path where they will meet characters both curious and disturbing. With intimate knowledge of the region, Parsley crafts a world where disaster and wonder coexist, blurring the lines between history and myth. Lovely, lush, and haunting."

—Alisa Alering, author of *Smothermoss*

"A surreal novella that grabs your hand and pulls you along for a deeply personal trek through childhood, loss and memory. Em J Parsley expertly captures stifling vignettes of the Appalachian summer, as uneasy and fragmented as the town of Mission itself. Haunting and as inescapable as the kudzu—will cling to you for days after reading."

—William A. Wellman, creator of *Hello From The Hallowoods*

YOU,
FROM
BELOW

YOU, FROM BELOW

A NOVELLA

EM J PARSLEY

Published by Split/Lip Press
PO Box 27656
Ralston, NE 68127
www.splitlippress.com

ISBN: 978-1-952897-42-9

Cover Art: Taken from ' To the River Plate and back : the narrative of a scientific mission to South America, with observations upon things seen and suggested' by W.J. Holland, 1913
Cover and Book Design: David Wojciechowski
Editing: Kate Finegan

TO YOUR HOME. MAY YOU HELP IT FLOURISH AND FLOURISH WITHIN IT IN RETURN.

I. COLLAPSE

You are climbing a mountain. There's an envelope in your hand. Behind you, where a valley and a town named Mission used to be, a crumbling pit smolders.

The earth swallowed Mission. It was like this: you sat on a hill after an unremarkable day of work, on the sturdy side of the county line, and watched in numb shock as the earth gave way beneath your home and consumed it with layers of echoing roars. There was no warning, unless you count the last thing your Mama said to you that morning.

You wonder, was the underbelly hollow this whole time? What was the final straw?

When you were a child, you used to spend every Saturday making mud pies in the front yard. Dozens of them, balanced along the chicken wire fence. Mama always said the two of you didn't need no dog with the way you dug up the yard to get your pie filling. If you had made one more pie, dug a little deeper, would your caked fingernails have carved empty air? A cavern? A boiling hell pit? Could you have popped a hole in Mission and collapsed it like a lung? Would you have been the first to fall into the deep?

These questions don't have answers.

You are climbing a mountain. There's an envelope in your hand. It's gonna get water damage, what with the way your hand's sweating. Best to put it in your jacket for safe keeping. When you stop to catch your breath, you have a desperate need to turn and look at Mission. Remind yourself of the loss. Like Lot's wife, except you've already turned back to look near on a dozen times now, and the only salt is in your sweat. So you turn without fear of transformation. You can't see any rubble. The hole is too deep, sinking into an abyssal blackness shaped in a ragged cutout of the town's borders.

You are climbing a mountain with a letter in your jacket pocket. You don't know how you know you're going the right way, but you are—doubt doesn't factor in. Your foot slips on a slick bit of mud, and you fall forward, nearly getting a face full. You catch yourself on your hands, and pain shoots up your left wrist. You're grateful you put the letter in your jacket. To ruin your purpose, and this early on in your journey, would be unthinkable. When you wipe the mud off your hands onto your sleeve, it smells like sulfur.

You are climbing a mountain, and the pain in your wrist has faded, probably. Probably. You can't feel it, anyway, and that must mean it's gone. The human body is not capable of unfelt pain.

You're in shock. There's no other explanation for a person who watches their home get swallowed whole, then finishes their lunch, wipes the dust off their glasses, and begins to climb a mountain. As you climb, you notice the lack of sirens in the distance. The sinking shook the entire valley, the shuffling sound of earth and rock and architecture all merging as they fell was louder than a coal mine collapse. And the *screaming*—there was pleading and praying and shrieking and surely folks heard that. As isolated as Mission was, there's no way its death went utterly unnoticed by all but you. And yet, no one comes. Maybe no one cares to come.

A thought crops up unbidden: maybe you don't care.

Well, that seems unlikely, you tell yourself. You must care—your Mama, your first love, the woman at the gas station who handed you your pack of cigarettes every morning whose name you suddenly cannot recall—you cared about them. No, you loved them, you're sure. You turn around to face it again, to prove to yourself, to make sure you suffer and feel. Sweat drips into your left eye; the salt burns. Dust rises from the pit. The cloud obscures the rest of the untouched valley, leaving only the destruction to witness. The dust coats the leaves on the trees around you. It coats your lips, your eyelashes, inside your nostrils.

Maggie, that was her name. See? You care.

You are climbing a mountain. There is a letter in your jacket. Your mother's last words sit in your chest: Careful out there today, alright? Swear to Jesus, this heat's gonna turn us all to dust.

II. "I HAVE A MESSAGE"

The envelope in your jacket pocket was not there when you woke up this morning, before your home was eaten by the earth. You're pretty sure it was not there on your way to work, or when you sat on that hill and watched Mission sink in on itself. But when you started climbing, there it was.

As you climb, you say, to nothing in particular, "I have a message." You don't know what's inside the envelope, so it's not *your* message, per se, but it's in your hands. You are its vessel.

Altitude has cleared the air a bit. The dust no longer clings to every available surface. A cottontail, sticking to honeysuckle shadows, eyes you as a predator. You share your thoughts merely because it's there to receive them: "I have a message." It looks at you expectant, untrusting, waiting to hear the message. "It's not for you," you clarify. The rabbit looks disappointed. You pat your pockets, thinking you'll give it something to eat to make up for your lack of urgent missives for it. You come up empty—you didn't bring food with you at all. There wasn't any left to bring, of course, and even if there had been, it's not like you had stuck around to find out. It's alright, though. You're not hungry. Maybe you should be, but it's a distant concern. The rabbit disappears into the brush, and you're sad to see it go. Its brief, wary company had stirred your senses.

When you were a kid back in Mission, you had a friend named Danny whom you did not love. They were nice enough—you enjoyed playing on their tire swing, and they had a sweet singing voice that lilted along the breeze in a soothing way. But you did not love them. Not for any particular reason, not because you were cruel or they were unlovable. It just didn't work. You liked them. You enjoyed them. You did not love them, not like they loved you.

Danny loved you with the kind of intensity and passion that adults think children are incapable of. It feels a little self-deprecating to say, but you never really understood why. You were not especially popular, nor good-looking, not the star of a sports team or lead in any of the school plays. You were just a kid who played in the mud on weekends and barely passed math tests and got up early on Tuesdays so you wouldn't miss your favorite cartoon. You did choir, because Danny asked you to do it with them and you felt you had said "no" to them too many times. Your singing voice wasn't anything special, not like theirs. But Danny looked at you with something approaching reverence. You were gospel to them.

Your ascent leads you up a gravel road that's been claimed by the surrounding wilderness. Someone must have lived up here once, a long time ago, but that time has passed. They'd have to hike down steep, untrodden masses of woods to get to Mission, and surely you would have noticed someone sojourning from the mountainside every so often to get supplies or seek out company. So you keep walking the gravel with the hope of finding an abandoned house or shed to take shelter in for the night.

Things had ended badly with Danny. That level of worship could never be healthy, and it had only escalated over the years. They asked you to prom. It was an earnest invitation, and well, you weren't going with anyone else, so you said yes. You still hadn't let yourself realize the extent of their devotion—either out of a lack of self-esteem or complete denial—and even as your other friends tried to tell you it would do more harm than good, you insisted it would be fine. Danny knew you were going as friends. They knew it wasn't like that.

They tried to kiss you at the end of the night, and only after you gently pushed them away and said, "no, thank you," very politely, as if they had asked if you take sugar in your tea, did you realize the depth of their love. In your teenage angst, you felt sure that this, right here, was the worst thing you'd ever done or would ever do to a person.

The two of you never spoke another word to each other—you only ever saw them slinking around the school halls between periods, and after you graduated, they slipped off your radar completely. Come to think of it, you hadn't seen them in years—not a glimpse of them across the grocery store or an awkward greeting at a baby shower—nothing. What had happened to them?

You know what's happened to them now, you suppose.

Further along the gravel, as it becomes nothing more than a thin trail of pebbles dodging between brambles and trees, a noise reaches your ears. At first, it's indistinguishable from the low-level ringing that's been plaguing you since Mission sank. But no, it's not that: there's a steady buzzing in the air.

A bee flicks past your face, startling you. Several more flit about only a couple feet in front of you, all coming from a single direction.

You've just decided to go around, no need to disturb the hive, when a voice filters through the trees. "Is anyone there?" It calls out.

You freeze. A bee lands on your arm, you brush it off.

The voice calls out again, "Hello?"

You push through the branches, curiosity overrunning fear, and see a figure standing alone in a clearing. Behind them stands an old sycamore with a bulging beehive weighing down one of its stark-white branches.

You would say they have a familiar face, because it feels true, but you can't actually see it. They wear a beekeeping suit with a wide-brimmed hat and a veil, but the veil is many-layered, long, tattered and tumbling down their front, strips of it going all the way down to their knees and fluttering about as they move towards you.

"Hello! Would you like some honey?" they ask, trilling voice piercing through their veil.

"No, thank you," you say. "I'm not hungry."

They tell you that it's good honey, right off the comb—they're a foot or two away from you now, bees trailing behind them in wandering arcs. Their outstretched white gloved hand grips a slab of dripping honeycomb. "It's good honey, honest," they assure you.

Again, you thank them, and tell them you're really not hungry.

The suit switches the comb to their left hand, grabs your hand with the sticky-fingered glove, and ushers you over to two falling-apart barrels and a massive tree stump that serve as a table and chairs. They slap a comb down on the stump in front of you and gesture for you to eat.

Once again: "I ain't hungry. Really."

The suit produces two chipped teacups, dribbles honey into both of them, and sets one down in front of you. The bees buzz around your head, one crawls up your neck; you brush it off. One lands on the corner of your mouth and startles you so badly that you slap it, and the bee stings your face.

The suit leaps up, spilling its cup of honey, and reaches out towards you, puffy gloves grabbing your chin and inspecting the sting. The touch feels electric in all the wrong ways—tingling, unwanted—you push the hands back, mumbling assurances that you're fine. The suit backs off, and the swarm retreats with it.

They tell you it won't happen again. "We'll fix this," they promise, gesturing behind you.

You look back and see, floating on the breeze—no, not on the breeze, being carried by the swarm—you see another beekeeper's veil. You realize what's going to happen a moment before it does, but you cannot move as the bees drop the veil over your face and the suit arranges it to hang properly. The world filters muzzy through the white mesh, your nose inches from the suit's own tattered veil as they continue to fuss over you.

When they seem satisfied, they sit back down on their side of the stump, righting the spilled cup of honey and lifting it to their face. They neither remove their veil nor slip their cup under the mesh to allow a sip; they press the cup to the outside of the veil where you would assume a mouth might be, and mime the act of drinking. The honey dribbles down the veil. They gesture towards your cup, and despite your constant assertions that you're not hungry, you don't feel as if you can refuse. You pick up the teacup, observing the bee perched on the rim. You don't want to brush it off, so you lift the cup, mimicking the suit's motions. The honey spills down your veil and onto your lap, and the suit nods in satisfaction, then gestures to the comb in front of you. This pantomime of domesticity scrapes shallowly into your gut, tries to dig further, and finds solid rock. Your Mama made you toast—butter, cinnamon, sugar—every morning until the morning you decided you were too big to have your Mama make your breakfast, at which point she graciously let you smush cold butter and unevenly melted cinnamon and sugar into your toast and hers.

You pick up the sticky comb, lift it to your veil, and feign eating. The suit continues to nod vigorously and do the same. You feel exiled from yourself. Your body mocks depth.

Trapped in this game of play-pretend, you raise the comb to your face again, and ask, "Do you live here by yourself?"

The suit shakes its head. "The bees are here."

Oh, there it is again—your insides scrape against shallow bedrock. It burns. You inquire, with candor, "Are you lonely?"

It giggles, and tells you that the bees, *of course,* the bees keep it company. "And now, you." It sounds delighted. "You will keep me company."

"I'll have to go, eventually," you say. "I can't stay forever."

The suit stills. Tilts its head and says, cheerful, assured, "Ohhh, you'll stay."

"What?"

"You know, you remind me of this boss I had, once. Real nice man. Everyone liked him. He was funny, people felt comfortable coming to him with their problems, he was always watching out for us. Just...just a real upstanding guy. It was backbreaking work, but someone's gotta do it, and we all worked as a team to get it done. Well—boss-man, he had to—he didn't do the work *with* us, of course." The suit laughs, high and jittery—*what a ridiculous idea,* the laugh says. "Someone has to be the one watching out for us all. But he was sympathetic, you know? He was always going on about how grateful he was to us, for all our hard work."

You pull the veil away from your face, just enough to catch a breath while they keep talking.

"And, oh! There was this lottery, right, where they would draw our names once a month, and whoever's name got drawn, they'd get a day off of their choosing the next month. Such a nice gesture." The suit pauses, watches bee alight on its glove, studies it. "It's funny—we all started to dread getting our name drawn—what if something happened while we were away, right? It seemed selfish to take time away when boss-man worked so tirelessly." The suit stretches, arms reaching up to the sky, before flopping back to their lap. They sigh. It's disconcertingly human.

"People stopped taking days off, even when their name was drawn. It just felt too important. But the gesture was still nice. It really was. The next time my name got drawn, I didn't even think of taking it. And the time after that, and after that—I just couldn't. It feels good, you know, to do work well and be rewarded for it."

You think of hot summer days spent removing barbed wire for neighbors, ripping out carpeting in Danny's dad's moldy double-wide. Satisfied sore muscles.

"After a while my wife, Lena, she started complaining, said I was never around. Said she missed me. I loved Lena so much—too good for me, ya know?—and so the next time my name got drawn, I told boss-man that I'd be taking the time. He looked disappointed, which was understandable. I hated to disappoint him. Real upstanding guy, ya know. Lena was so excited, though. We had a whole day, just for us. We had a picnic, and we walked around town, just taking in the sights. I tried to enjoy it, but the whole time I just kept thinking about what if they needed me, and I wasn't there?"

The suit picks up their cup, takes another imaginary sip. A glob of honey lands on a bee crawling up their suit, trapping it—its little legs flail in slow motion. You watch the bee suffocate, thinking about alerting the suit to its plight, but you don't, and you're not sure why.

"They replaced me. Came in the next day to find some other guy doing the work. Boss-man said he hoped I understood—I was just so integral to the operations that when I was gone for the day, they couldn't really do it without me, so they hired a new guy. I get it, really. Makes sense. I shouldn't have—well. No hard feelings. He even said he'd call me if something opened up. Real upstanding guy, right? I'm sure he'll call soon."

You can't peel your eyes off the bee, buried under the amber honey. Your head feels fuzzy. You can't bring yourself to console.

"Anyway, you're here now, so you can help me with this work until bossman calls me, can't you? Oh, look at that! You've already got a veil. Perfect. It's good to be prepared."

"Listen," you start. Your voice sounds far too close among these layers, bouncing back and filling up the air. "I really have to go. I have a message I have to deliver."

The suit freezes. "Is the message for me?" It asks, full of hope.

"No," you say. And then, because it seems right, you add, "I'm sorry."

They lean across the stump, face close to yours, and if you could see their expression you know it would be pleading. You try to peer past the veil, glimpse anything beyond the layers of mesh, but there's too much. And while there's definitely something moving behind all that covering, you can't make out any facial features.

They ask again, heedless, "Is the message for me? Please, please—is it for me? Is it from him? What does it say?"

"It's not for you," you repeat. The buzzing becomes louder, fills the air. It's hard to hear your own voice over the sound. It's almost nice—a respite from the emptiness of your thoughts.

"Why not?" they beg. "Why isn't it for me? Why don't I deserve to hear it?"

"It's not about deserving," you try to say.

"Then what is it about?" they want to know. "What do I have to do?"

You need them to understand. There's nothing they can do. The message isn't for them, and it isn't for you, and that's all there is to it.

"What do I have to do?" they repeat. "What do I have to do?" The suit shakes you by the shoulders, and the bees crawling over their hands cross over onto your jacket.

"Nothing," you tell them. This truth, ripped open like a secret, hangs limply in the air. "There's nothing, I'm sorry." You try to break away, but their grip is tight.

Your face throbs where the bee stung it, and the feeling spreads across your cheek and down your neck. You feel dizzy, numb, and the only thing keeping you present is the sound of buzzing. It fills you, all-consuming. It hurts. It *burns*. If you don't leave, it will take up residence within, expanding until nothing else remains.

You have already lost nearly everything, and for a moment, you wonder if one last act of losing yourself would be so bad. It's tempting to fall into the overwhelming noise. To let it take you. But you cannot be a vessel for both the buzzing and the message, and you must deliver the message.

"I have a message," you mumble, but it doesn't make it past the veil. Your slow body begs you to give in—surely it would be easier. You stagger to your feet, fumbling for the veil, but you can't get a grip on it. One step, if you take one step, you'd be—you trip on the gauze trailing from the veil down to the earth, and it gets ripped from your head with a sharp pain to your neck.

"I have—" you gasp as the clarity hits you, and you stand again, shaking. "I'm sorry, I'm sorry. I have a message. I have a message."

As you flee the clearing, the suit's voice turns to static, and becomes one with the buzzing bees.

III. KUDZU HELD HER

Despite growing up right on the mountain's base, touching it, living in tandem with it your entire life, you never explored anything beyond where the valley meets the rise. You wandered the hills below, knew every inch of the valley itself, but that was all. Maybe if you had someone braver than you to explore it with—but you didn't, so you remained unlearned in the mountain's secrets.

The closest you ever got was the woods at the base, and even then only once, when you were no older than ten or eleven and spending the day at your Gran's. Gran lived on the other side of Mission, which wasn't far, all things told, but you only visited a couple times a year, and she never came to see you in the trailer park. Her house, crowded with pictures of people whose names you didn't know, sat on the edge of the woods. Your Mama dropped you off, waving to Gran from the car as Gran watched from the porch, raising a single hand in stony greeting.

Your Gran had always been a disapproving presence. She thought you were strange, with no significant talent or beauty to excuse it. She blamed this strangeness on your Mama, and was plenty vocal about it. Mama bore this patiently, as she bore seemingly everything, taking the constant criticisms from the mother of her long-gone boyfriend with a smile that never cracked.

On the day you went into the woods, Gran watched TV in the living room, having given you explicit orders to only bother her when it was time for dinner. Happy to obey, you slipped out and turned her yard into a series of holes from which mud pies could be gleaned. She didn't notice when you stole her aluminum pie tins (and one very pretty ceramic one) from the kitchen cabinets.

The cat came from under the fence—a fat, tortoise-shell creature, trotting up to you like an old friend, sniffing your muddy hand with interest. You had never owned any pets and most people at the trailer park kept dogs over cats, so when you reached out towards the cat in childish delight, you gripped it around the middle too eagerly, and it yowled, flailed out of your grasp, then darted off towards the woods. You were up and after it immediately, ducking under the fence and stumbling through uncut brush without a second thought.

The heavily canopied woods made it difficult to see; you tripped over a root, caught yourself in the dirt, and sat there for a moment, catching your breath and glowering at the perpetrator, only looking up when you heard a rustling and remembered your purpose.

You noticed the cat crouched in the corner of your vision only after you saw this: a woman, towering a couple feet in front of you, her concerned tone reaching past your disorientation at her sudden appearance, "Are you okay?" It was too dark to see her lips move. "Here, let me help you up, poor baby."

The woman's head dipped forward and hinged on her neck like a lead pendulum. Her long arms swayed and twisted—you couldn't tell where her fingers ended and the shadows and leaves began—they strained infinitely towards you, intent unknown. Every fireside ghost story you'd insistently been too brave to be scared of came rushing back all at once as the extension of her hand passed over the cat. She was speaking again, though you couldn't make out any words this time, not with all your attention on the vine, the shadow, her hand. She touched your arm. You shrieked and ran.

Years later you realized, of course, that the woman was, in fact, just a woman. Shadows and imagination do funny things to children's heads. The Appalachian Trail wasn't too far off from your town and hikers got lost sometimes. She probably found her way to the gas station that afternoon and got herself set right again.

At the time, however, your encounter with a woodland monster had left you inconsolable. Your Gran received your screaming and crying with frustrated indifference, scolding you for tracking mud on your shoes and making a scene. You flung yourself at her, pudgy little hands gripping tight, and she pried you off her as one removes pilling from a sweater, handing you a handkerchief to sop up your snotty face while she called your Mama, demanding she come and deal with "the child." That night you sat on the couch, held by your Mama, as she rubbed your shoulders and said, "You know, sometimes it's hard for people to know how to be kind. They don't always know what that looks like. Your Gran don't know what kindness looks like, and that's very sad for her, and it's very sad for you." It took a while for you to be invited back to Gran's.

Your climb up the mountain brings you to a bald. Vines cover the grass and stretch beyond the bald to a dense, tangled canopy. You feel none of the residual fear that your childhood encounter left you with—that low, gut-deep dread you used to get when you glimpsed your long shadow in the moonlight, a spike of anxiety at the sight of a streetlamp that had been taken over by kudzu—it's been replaced by numb acceptance. You move forward, only slowing your gait to take care not to trip over roots and brush.

When the woman who is not a woman comes to you, it feels natural. She has always been there, waiting for you, and you for her. How nice, to be anticipated. To be wanted.

She's draped in kudzu, more vine than woman and more trustworthy smile than vine, and she promises one thing and one thing only: embrace. You follow her. Of course you do. You know you have a message to deliver, but it can wait. Surely, with an offer like that, it can wait.

She leads you away from the narrow animal trail you were following, deeper into the woods. You chase after that smile, her promise. As she walks ahead of you, she tells you the story of how she came to be. It sits right with you. Perhaps it's your story, too.

"I planted my children around my home," she tells you. Her voice rasps and rustles in her throat. "Just as a pretty little decoration to distract from the paint color. He had painted the house this sickly, dying yellow that I couldn't stand. I told him I didn't like the color, but he didn't care. He never cared. I was cautious with the children, at first. New motherhood, you know. Trimming them. Telling them where they can and can't grow. But after a while, it seemed...cruel. To restrict them. So I tried to step back and let them thrive on their own.

"He hated it," she hums, indifferent. "Told me to get it under control. To do my duty as a wife and take care of our home, 'sweetheart.' He always called me that. Sweetheart. I didn't like it. I've always thought 'dear' sounded so much more sincere, don't you?"

You nod. You think about your Gran, and how much better it would have been if she had called you "dear," even once.

"I did what he said, for a little while. He had this way about him that made him hard not to listen to. His voice was so soft and gentle-like, but his words were made of steel. And yet every time I went out there with my clippers, it felt like cutting off pieces of me. So they grew. They grew up and over the windows, to the roof, covering every bit of that nasty yellow. And when I was inside their embrace, tucked in the home they had claimed—Lord, there was nothing like it. Just...silence. And stillness. And safety.

"To think—*ha*—to think he ever thought he could control us. It was the last thing he tried to do, you know. Took a machete to the children and started hacking—barely made a dent, the silly little man. But we were never going to let him get far.

"It's funny, isn't it? That everyone thought he was such a kind man because he knew the talk. They never understood, though. Soft talkin' is a wretched cacophony in comparison to total, blissful quiet." She pauses. Closes her eyes, and beckons you to do the same. She's right—the quiet is blissful.

"Anyways," she continues, "we consumed him. While he was hacking away uselessly, I called him inside the house for a nice glass of ice water, and then we grew over the doors, and he couldn't get out. I stood outside, listened to him yell and scream, but he was so muffled by the layers of my precious children that I could barely hear him. I just...sat against the door and let myself be swaddled as they contracted around his throat and suffocated him." She smiles. Her teeth lengthen in the shadow. "I do wonder if it was quiet for him, at the end. I hope not."

She pulls you through the trees, her hand wraps around yours, and the pressure around your palm is understanding, that of someone who would never let you go. "We didn't stay there, in the yellow house. It was time to build a home of our own, one where we could live without restraint." She gestures to the vine-hooded canopy. "Isn't it perfect?"

The vines cover everything. It's difficult to tell what was once hidden beneath. And it's perfect, it really is.

"Dear," she says. "Do you wish to feel our embrace?"

The briefest of hesitations—you have a message, after all—gets overrun by the thought of home and the chasm in your chest that's been there since the collapse. The possibility of that void being filled drives you towards her.

You smile. She squeezes your hand.

As you move deeper into the forest's fold, the kudzu rushes towards her as children do to a loving parent. They use her ankles as purchase to climb up her legs until she doesn't so much walk as sway vaguely forwards, like an autumn leaf succumbing to gravity. They continue to envelop her, creeping up her torso, towards her chin.

She greets them with unmitigated joy, calls them by name. Her speech is clear and strong even as the vines snake into her mouth and down her throat, but you realize you can't hear her voice—she doesn't have a voice, not like yours. There's nothing but the sound of leaves brushing against leaves, a constant, quiet whisper that goes beyond language, and yet you understand. You understand every millimeter of the kudzu's draped growth over slumping, resigned trees, reverberating from the roots, up through the dirt. Voices breach obscenity when communion like this exists.

Now the leaves cover her fully; now her face is a comforting mass of green, pulsing life; now she rocks forward to take both your hands in hers; now the hands holding yours are vines that wrap around each of your fingers, your palms, and grip your wrists with firm surety; now the vine climbs up your arms, encases your ribcage. This is very nearly it.

"My dear," she whispers in the tongue of a thousand spreading branches, "You are welcome here."

When she pulls you in, all is silent for just a moment. The embrace is firm, tight, and—you are sure—never-ending. It reminds you of your Mama, but without the fear that you've disappointed her, that she resents you, that you take up too much space, or not enough. This is how your Gran was supposed to hold you. This is how every touch you've ever experienced should have been.

And then it shifts, tightens, and continues to tighten. It pins your arms to your sides and spreads itself across your chest and around your torso. You cannot, you realize, embrace in return.

When the vines get to your mouth, it occurs to you that you don't want to be held. She envelops you tenderly, she rustles and shushes you—*sh, sh*—she wants your stillness, she thinks your stillness must mean your peace. What else could stillness mean? A tree arrested by the kudzu feels secure in its final grasp. Yes, its hold will eventually kill, but something must, so why shouldn't it be this?

She asks you, "Don't you want to die at home, cradled?"

You do, but she doesn't understand that this isn't your home. She doesn't understand that you must keep moving. Something tugs in your stomach, tickles at the base of your throat. Vines crawl up your throat and out your mouth; they brush against your teeth. They say, *sh, sh. Be still. Shhh.*

Is this a kindness? you wonder. When she embraces you, she just wants your safety. There are worse things to want, and worse ways to kill. If you could speak, and you cannot, you would ask her, do you think this is kindness? Do you know kindness?

And if she wished to respond, and she would not, she would say, *what is kindness?*

This is nothing like your Mama, and you feel ashamed that you ever thought so. Mama's hugs were soft, like her voice, and when you were little and squirmed out of her grip, she let you go without hesitation, kissing you on your part as you went.

As the vines fill your lungs, you think, *this is not kind. I wish I could have explained what kindness is.*

But still, you're glad she's holding your hand.

IV. THE RAPTURE

When you awaken, your throat is raw and your chest feels as if it could float away without you. There's too much air and too much space. You stand, check your pocket. The message remains. It demands that you move.

You don't know how long you've been going when you find yourself, suddenly, as if you'd been dropped there by providence, in the middle of an abandoned town. Well, not quite abandoned. It doesn't look like it's fallen apart, it looks—demolished, perhaps. Massive patches of torn-up dirt dot each side of the street, an occasional stone chimney remains, foundations, a single brick wall harkens to the ghostly presence of a home, but the remaining pieces don't look weathered. You feel pretty sure that it's early fall now—there's the beginning of a chill in the air and the trees have begun to turn—but this place looks like it has just received a heavy summer rain. Rivulets of muddy water trickle down the single dirt road that runs through the center of the town.

You come upon the clapboard front wall to a church with two empty doorframes side-by-side, leading to open air. You step through one of the doors onto the dirt on the other side, noting the stone foundation in a rectangle where the rest of the church used to be.

Your Mama was a devoted church-goer—brushed your hair and put you in something clean every Sunday to make the ten-minute walk to the ratty old chapel that made its home between the trailer park and struggling cattle farms. She sang the hymns with precision, listened to the sermon like an attentive student. This ritual was neither important nor upsetting to you, even when you got bored enough to slump all the way down in the pew and imagine figures out of the knots in the wooden ceiling beams. The preacher was nice—what was his name? Elijah? Ezekiel? Something preacher-y. When you were little and came up to the front to take communion, he always crouched down to meet your eyes and smile at you, *body of Christ,* as he gave you your wafer.

He preached on nice things, mostly. Loving your neighbor, loving God, thanking God for the good things you had, feeling bad about the bad things you did but good about the fact that Jesus loves and forgives you. Give to the poor. It's unclear who that message was for, since most of the folks here *were* the poor that should be given to. Money tended to run a neat little loop—paltry tithes of what people could afford got put in the church community fund, which was then used to buy canned food for single-parent households or do home repairs after storms.

When your grandpa died, you and your Mama got an invitation to go have dinner with the preacher and his wife and kids. You remember thinking his daughter was very pretty, and that you'd like to be her friend, and you remember trying very hard not to look at her the whole night. You wish now, with a pang like an infected and ignored splinter, that you had befriended her. It would hurt more if you had, but still.

Beyond the church, you see a single building still intact—a schoolhouse. Sitting on the steps up to the schoolhouse is a woman. You wave, and she remains still. You approach. She stares past you. You're not sure she knows you're there.

"What happened here?" you ask.

"They left," she mumbles, arms wrapped around her stomach. "Rain falls up. They left."

"I don't understand," you admit.

This phrase triggers a reaction in the woman. She gains a semblance of clarity and grabs your hand, pulling you over to the steps. She sits, dragging you down with her.

"I'll explain. I'll teach you. Then you'll understand. I can teach you. I can teach you." Without waiting for a response, she tells you her story.

"I came here on a missions trip when I was just eighteen. They needed me to teach their children. They were such good children, but so uneducated, you know? It wasn't their fault, of course, and I was determined that they would be reading and writing like nobody's business by the time I left. I spent a year teaching them. It was hard work, but it was rewarding. God had sent me here to help, I could feel it. I taught them good grammar and good speaking. I taught them the value of hard work." The woman's eyes lose focus as she says this. "God rewards hard work, I told them. There's nothing The Lord Our God won't do for you if you show your dedication and love for Him."

She nods her head, sharp, confirming this internal truth. "When my year was up, I didn't want to leave. I still had *so much* to teach, and—and I had fallen in love. With the preacher. John. So I stayed, and I taught. I taught them to do their numbers, and I taught them the history of the founding of our great nation. They were such good students. Stubborn, sometimes, in their ways, their traditions, but I was getting through to them, I could feel it. And so was John. He was an outsider too, you know. Placed here right out of seminary, and already doing *such* good work. I think that's where our connection began. The people here, well, I love them, but they're suspicious of outsiders. John and I bonded over the difficulties of trying to get through to them. We were married a year and a half after I came here.

"John had felt a calling to straighten out the differences between myth and Biblical teaching. These people…they have so many superstitions, so many funny little rituals. Some of them are harmless, I suppose, but some…." She sighs. "There was a witch. Her name was Meabh. I had heard stories before coming here. I had read about the sorcerers and court magicians in the Bible, I'd even heard fellow missionaries' stories of people in foreign countries who can do black magic and such, so it's not that I didn't believe in that sort of thing, but it had all seemed distant. Fairy-tale-like."

When the woman dragged you down with her, you had ended up in a crouch. It wasn't uncomfortable—*it should be*, something at the base of your neck says. Your calves should be burning. You think about it so hard that you're unsure if you've tricked yourself into imagining discomfort—you shift to sit with your knees pulled to your chest on the step below her. She plows ahead.

"Meabh was proof, though. That the devil gives his power to those who crave it. I tried to minister to her at first, I really did, but she always said, *I know Jesus, Miss. He and I are good and well acquainted, and He accepts all my activities, don't you worry none.*

"When I was pregnant with my first child, Meabh came to me and said she should be there for its birth, that there was going to be trouble but she could help. I asked her how she knew this, of course, and she said *God* had told her. I laughed at the idea and told her God had told *John* of no such thing, nor myself, and that we would be just fine with the town doctor. She frowned and nodded and said, *You think I'm working for the devil, Miss, but our Gods are the same. Ain't a lick 'a difference.*

"We lost the first child. But the Lord blessed us with a second, and a third, and a fourth, and throughout it all I knew, felt the conviction in my very soul, that Meabh's presence would not have helped. She had been sent by Satan as a temptation, and I had resisted. We cannot understand God's reasons, but we can follow his commands faithfully."

The woman stares into the middle distance, eyes roving over the torn-up earth. You think she's forgotten you're there. "Six months ago," she continues, "Meabh knocked on our door after dinner. I had nearly forgotten about her—it had been years since we last spoke, and I had heard rumors that she hardly left her home anymore. She did not look well. She had lost weight, and her eyes had turned sunken and tired. I couldn't help but think she looked more satanic than ever.

"She had come to talk to John this time. John was always gracious with the flock, even the ones who had strayed, so he invited her in and sat her down. I ushered the children off to sleep, hushing their questions about *Miracle Meabh*. When I returned to the kitchen, she was rambling utter incoherence about the rain—the rain, she said, was coming and it would either wash us all away or take us with it, but we had to prepare.

"John asked what she meant by *take us with it*, and she just shook her head and mumbled, *Rain falls up. Rapture. Rain falls up.* She was clearly unwell. If it were not for the fact that I knew that demons can only be invited into the soul of the unsaved, and that I knew she had been given plenty opportunities to be saved in her life, I think I would have felt bad for her. John thanked her for her warning, promised he would pray about it, and then stood to lead her out. *You don't believe me,* she gasped, clinging to the kitchen table as if we were going to drag her out by her boots. *I believe you have been spoken to,* John assured her. *I will pray.* Meabh turned to me, desperation in her hollow eyes. *I was right about your child, you know I was. Please.* She did not look like a liar. She looked scared. I did not cave to Satan's temptation."

You have known people like this woman; fervor like hers was the cause of your drifting. When you were sixteen, you officially stopped attending church. You had assumed this would be a problem for your Mama, given her track record of devotion, but she just frowned, then nodded, contemplative. D*o you believe in something?* she had asked.

You shrugged. *I dunno, Mama.*

I would like it if you believed in something. Doesn't have to be this, but—just something. Helps you keep going.

Alright, Mama.

Can't make you, she assented. *That ain't belief. But I'd like it if you'd think about it.*

You promised to think about it.

Now, you bite your lip to keep yourself from admonishing this woman; desire to hear the story outweighs the judgment you cast on her.

"Over the next couple of months, Meabh returned to the community, but not as the miracle-worker that people knew her as. She stood on the main road at all hours, sometimes from dawn to dusk, begging to be heard, repeating, sometimes chanting, *Rain falls up, rapture, rain falls up.* At first, people regarded her with something like pity. She was loved, despite her oddities. People trusted her. And now they were seeing her true nature. I'll admit, I felt a little vindicated to see her fall like this. But I told myself, no, one must show mercy to everyone. One must show love, even. I tried to bring her food once. She thanked me, and refused to eat it. I wasn't going to waste anything on her ungratefulness after that.

"After a couple weeks of Meabh's ranting, things started to shift. It was the children who first started listening to her. Eliza, one of my more stubborn students, sat down in front of her one day, in the middle of the street, and started listening, properly, as if Meabh was telling a hearth story. When Meabh realized Eliza was there, she addressed her directly. Eliza asked questions. Meabh lit up and babbled at her some more. Honest to God, I don't even know what she said, what the rest of her insights were beyond *rain falls up*. Simon, the MacLeods' boy, was next. He sat next to Eliza, asking no questions but staring up at Meabh with his hands quiet in his lap. Then it was Mary, always a troublemaker in my class. She hopped from one foot to the other while she listened, but she listened nonetheless. One by one, out of curiosity, courage, or peer-pressure, the children gathered to listen to Meabh.

"Jealousy burned me up. After everything, after years and years of living in this *nothing* town,"—she spits out *nothing* like it's worse than nothing—"after giving up all I had to minister to these people, the children sat quietly and listened to Meabh as if she had wisdom. John was worried, but I could also tell he was doubting. I tried not to feel disgusted with him, tried to follow his example, but where was his conviction? Was he going to cave to every false prophet and rambling idiot who sowed seeds of dissent?"

Your Mama's question of belief crawls up from where it had hidden in your subconscious for over a decade. You want to ask this woman, *what do you believe in?*

"Folks began putting up sandbags around their homes, and when I asked what for, they told me that Meabh said that the rain's gonna fall down for a while before it falls up, and that we should be prepared. One day, I came home from teaching and found John fortifying our home for a flood. I was absolutely furious, but he just looked tired. He told me it couldn't hurt to be prepared, said surely it wasn't worth risking the children.

"That's what broke me. I woke up the next day and walked out into the street, Bible in hand, opposite to Meabh, and began to preach. I preached on hypocrisy and the ways in which Satan disguises himself as the familiar and friendly. A couple of the children migrated over to me, three of whom were my own, all of them occasionally glancing back at Meabh to witness her delirium. I preached to them their stubbornness, I exposed the way they clung to their tradition over the Word of God, I rebuked their mulish ignorance. The angrier I got, the more my preachings shifted from rebukes of the town to rebukes of Meabh—I spoke to her directly, demanded she repent of her sin, confess her place as a false prophet and servant of Hell. When I addressed her, she went quiet for the first time in weeks. She watched me, seeming to truly listen. Then she crossed the street and sat in front of me like one of the children. I had gotten through to her; I thought, *surely this is my moment of victory*. She beckoned for me to sit in the dirt across from her, and I felt compelled to listen, though I did not stop my sermon. We sat facing each other, knees touching, as I begged her to leave her sin behind. She stared into my eyes, nodding slowly, and then she reached out and placed her hands to caress my face. Only then did I stop speaking, locked into her gaze. Tears spilled down her cheeks, and her tears glowed with a golden light. When she opened her mouth, the same glow spilled from her lips. *You do not have permission to continue onwards*, she whispered. *Your journey ends here, in the in-between.* I told her that Hell had a space waiting for her unless she repented."

The woman runs like a recording. You feel alone, though you could reach out and touch her.

She goes on, "Meabh sighed and mumbled, with words like—like a trickling brook, *It's like I said. There ain't no difference between above and below.* And when I went to have a response to that, I found that I could not speak. My words had left me.

"I didn't want to go home. I couldn't stand to see John or the children, so I went to the schoolhouse. It began to rain that night and continued into the morning. No one showed up for school. I almost went home, but I still couldn't speak a word, and the thought of seeing John's doubting face was enough to keep me in the schoolhouse all day. By the second day, going home wasn't an option. The rain had flooded the road completely. On the third day, the waters began creeping up towards the schoolyard. I took to sitting by the window, watching the rapids churn towards the building's foundation. I felt a sense of peace in those couple of days. I felt sure my soul was about to be surrendered to God, and that Meabh would have her answer on above and below soon enough.

"On the seventh day, I awoke to the sound of rain gone, but when I opened the door to see if it had stopped, it hadn't. The water lapped at the doorway. I stared through the rain and the waters, and then I realized what was wrong—there were no droplets hitting the water. My eyes adjusted and I knew, of course. The rain was falling up. And then I looked out over the entire town, and saw that where homes and barns and stores had once been, there was nothing. Everything was *gone*. Not swept away—gone." She sucks in a sharp breath. "It was only then that I became afraid. The doubt washed over me and consumed my thoughts for a whole day while I watched the water get called back up into the heavens. And then, that night, in the midst of feverish prayers, I realized with relief and a sense of shame that this was another test. Like Job, my everything had been taken away, but I could not despair. This is part of God's plan, of course. *Of course*. All according to His will."

The woman repeats this phrase under her breath a couple times, and then goes quiet. She stares into the distance. She sits and she waits. As per the plan. All according to His will.

The breeze blows in her straw-blonde hair, and as you come back to your body at the end of her tale, you impulsively check the sky for storm clouds. It is clear.

Both left behind, abandoned to your solitudes—you feel as if you should have a connection with her. And yet you can't help but think, *why is she the one who gets to tell this story?* She hasn't the right. She taught them to read and then stole their words and made a home atop their tongues. They are gone—for better or worse—and only she remains to speak for them.

"I've worked hard," she says to the air. "I remain faithful. I will be rewarded. I will be rewarded."

You won't, you want to say. But you don't want to be the one to break her, even with all her wrongdoings stacking up against her. It doesn't feel like your right. Or maybe you think the real punishment would be to sit and wait and wait and wait for an eternity that is never going to come, wasting the little eternity she has now.

You leave her in her hopes without saying goodbye. She does not notice as you ascend further up into the mountain.

V. THE LANDSLIDE

You rise further, stepping into the crispness of late autumn. The trees around you shift—you notice it on the air before anything else: the cool, bright smell of pines—then the ground beneath you, fewer dead leaves than brown needles and moss. You've not been traveling long enough for the seasons to be moving in the way they are, but that doesn't change the facts. The letter in your jacket is a little warped now. You've stopped pulling it out to look; you're afraid of damaging it. Instead you peer into your pocket to make sure the letter's still there, and leave it be.

The brightness of the scent twists sharp—something rotten. An animal's carcass? Should it smell that rank in the cold? It's difficult to keep track of *shoulds*.

You find yourself, without wanting or meaning to, thinking of your first and only partner, Annie. You didn't date that long, you're not positive you were ever in love with her, but as you climb you miss her with an abrupt, absurd sharpness. She was kind, and she didn't mind that you didn't ever want to do much of anything. She sat next to you at the top of the hill overlooking Mission and seemed to understand that you didn't enjoy talking. And...

that's all you can remember about her. That's it. She was kind, she was quiet, her name was Annie. Why did you break up? Did she get bored of you? Did you get bored of *her?* What did she look like? She smiled a lot, probably. She was smarter than you but she never made you feel dumb, probably. Your Mama liked her, probably. That one's a safe bet—your Mama made an effort to like most everyone, and she wanted you to be happy.

You're too busy trying to conjure up more information about Annie to notice what you're coming up on until you're right up on it. A home, built on stilts into the side of the mountain. It's massive, and sturdy-looking too. Its timber frame has weathered with age, but there are no signs of corrosion.

On the porch that overlooks the mountainside, a woman sits with her legs dangling off the edge. She's so still that you believe she's a statue—and then she blinks and looks down at you. When she greets you, her voice cracks, as if she hasn't spoken in a long time. She beckons you to come up, and you accept the invitation as if it came from an old friend, climbing the stairs that lead from a flat landing to the porch. Once you reach the top you hesitate, self-conscious, but she pats the space next to her, so you sit and look out at the sunset. From this view you can see a town below. You didn't pass through this town to get here, but there it is.

Time moves slow, encased in amber. When she speaks, she startles you. "You're not from here," she says.

You concede to that truth, and she seems relieved.

"Is this your home?" you ask.

She nods, then goes very still again. You replicate her stillness, not wanting to disturb this scene. Only the setting sun remains in motion.

By the time she speaks again, the mountain sits in dull, gray light, and a fog is moving in. "There was a landslide," she tells you. "Long before I was born. It happened at night, and the home built on this spot slid down the mountain right along with the mud and trees. There was an entire family asleep in that home, and not one of them survived.

"No one wanted this land, after that. Some said it was cursed. Others said that the landslide was intentional, that the townsfolk had thought the family didn't belong and needed to be gotten rid of." She shrugs. "My grandpa didn't believe in all that, and he knew how to make something that would last. He bought the land and built this home, with rooms enough for as many grandchildren and great-grandchildren as he could think of, propped up with oak and built into a foundation of limestone. Grandpa always said that this house ain't goin' nowhere, not as long as our family's a family."

Her home was spacious and crowded and bustling, as a family home should be. She spent her childhood here, safe and loved, suspended above their little town with the confidence of a child who believes in the immortality of herself and everyone around her.

You understand this—the confidence, and what happens when it's broken—and you can't stop yourself from studying her face, dark and round with a halo of curls. She is, you believe, very pretty. She senses your eyes on her, turns her head to return your gaze with such intensity that it tears something inside you asunder. It's been so long since someone looked at you at all, much less in the way she's looking at you now, like pain is worth sharing.

She goes quiet again while the fog continues to take over, and then skips to the inevitable: she's the only one left. One mundane tragedy after the next—a heart attack took her grandpa, old age her grandma, an infection after a sawmill accident did Cousin Henry in, overdose claimed sister Mary, on and on, until it was just her and her uncle, who died in a car crash a while back. Throughout the emptiness, the gnawing loneliness, her home endured eternal, but it was different now. What was once a place where people gathered to eat and sleep and live, generation to generation, had calcified into an impotent shrine—lasting and inert. Still, she never considered selling it, moving away, even after the residents of the town began to turn on her. Her gaze on you doesn't waver throughout; she sits, back straight, hands unmoving, scanning you continually as if doing an inventory: eyes, hair, lips, jacket, hands, boots—checking for something. You let her look.

Lumber towns tend to empty out once they're past their relevance—children move away, parents retire, live in relative comfort, and die. Their children come to collect their photographs and dishes and leave the homes for rodents and birds to claim until they wilt into their own foundations. That's not what happened here. The lumber company stopped replenishing the trees—depleted soil, they said, the pines were rotting even as they grew, wood was useless—sawmills shut down, layoffs kept coming in big swaths until not a single person was left employed. And yet, people stayed. People festered. The homes and stores and churches began their journey to deterioration—vines grew up, broken windows sat unreplaced, upkeep on sagging cedar roofs and cracked mortar fell to the wayside, and no one seemed to care. The elderly died, the young had children, the children grew up in homes with tree roots breaching the floors, spending their nights listening to the possums skitter through their shattered windows and rustle around their kitchen.

The woman tells you that sometimes, she would see the townsfolk and there would be a moment, just a moment, where their faces would turn gaunt and she was sure that she had seen a beetle crawl into an empty eye socket. A child washed some mud off their hands in the river, and when they rubbed their palm, the skin peeled away, translucent white and waterlogged.

People who used to regard her genially, who gave her a dollar for ice cream as a child and told her to reach out if she needed anything after each increasingly-expected death, began to look at her sideways. As if she was the strange one. The grocer's comments on her unhealthy eating habits slipped from concern to disgust. When he snarled at her, the grimace split his face from lip to ear and a mixture of blood and yellow puss leaked from the crack. Her mother's friend's comments about finding her a boyfriend, once teasing and well-meaning, now held an air of judgment and suspicion, and when deflections were no longer enough, the friend's voice took on a wheezing, croaking quality until one day, in the midst of a tirade of recriminations, their voice gave out. They gasped as a lump traveled up their throat, and then they coughed up a baseball-sized mound of rotting flesh.

She knows, with a sudden jolt of lonely, lonely fear, that they are looking at her as if she does not belong here. She realizes the grocer is not the one from her childhood. She does not know this man. He has the same name—his son, of course. Or could it be his grandson? Certainly not.

Funeral after funeral trudged through the cemetery—they seemed daily, but the population did not dwindle. Reproduction kept pace with decay.

She pauses, and the pause lasts so long that you wonder if that's where the story ends. When she looks at you again, she searches for something in your face. You don't think she finds what she's looking for. And then she sighs, and explains to you softly, carefully, as if saying it is the last step to making it true, that she is lasting, and they will all eventually die. She has known this for a while now. The inevitable end that came for her family is not coming for her. She waited for it for a long while. After her uncle died, she figured it was only a matter of time before something simple and unavoidable claimed her, too. Pneumonia, perhaps. But she had never been prone to illness. So maybe an accident: an icy bridge, car tumbling over the rails that should have been replaced years ago. But she had always been the careful sort—never even broken a bone. A bizarre coincidence would be the way she'd go, then: she felt sure she would fall asleep down by the river and drown in a flash flood. The waters would carry her away and no one would ever find her body. But she knows better now.

As she walks through town, she notices a collection of rusting cars parked outside the community center. A sound comes from inside, like screaming, but lower. She almost thinks she's imagined it. She shouldn't investigate, but it's not like whatever it is will kill her, so she walks in, and every eye in town turns to her. Their mouths are open as if they no longer possess the muscles it would take to close them, and they are dead. Skulls peeking through thin, dry hairlines, insects crawling through the holes in their threadbare clothes. A crow perched on the mayor's arm—the bird pecks at a bit of exposed flesh on his collar bone. The raspy screams emanate from the holes in their exposed throats, modulating tones like a collection of discordant flutes. No, they're not screaming—they're singing. Their eyes, for those who still have eyes, accuse her of trespassing. She is not supposed to be here.

They do not want her here. She nods once, closes the door, and leaves.

"Do you know what the strangest thing is?" She asks you.

You do not.

"They seem happy. They're a community. They're together." She looks at you again, again, searching still. For happiness, maybe? You hope not. She won't find any. "They are full and rotting and together, and I...I won't die," she says with absolute surety in her voice. "This home is decaying, I can feel it. Its foundation is cracking, of course, but the roof will go first. It will sink in the middle, like a sigh. The damp, the rot, will weigh it down with no relief. The floors will be the next to fall. Hardwood, cut by my grandfather, perfect and unerring, houses worms. The worms' tunnels will become too numerous, and they will collapse the floor, hungry to claim. When the foundation finally cracks and my home falls, I'll be here, and I'll fall with it, but still I won't die.

"They'll come for me then, when my home can no longer keep them out. They'll come with maggots. The maggots will sing. They will want my body, but it's not theirs." She looks up at you, wistful. "Not mine either," she says.

There's a rumble behind the two of you. She hums. "There goes the roof. When the foundation collapses, you'll run." It's not a command, but it is a statement.

A crawling sensation travels from the base of your skull down your spine and gets trapped in your frantic ribcage.

"Come with me," you say, surprising yourself. You've never been much for companionship—too involved—but she feels steady like marble, and you suddenly believe yourself to be on the verge of collapse.

She smiles at you. Her teeth are sun-bleached white. "I wish I could."

Pleading, "You can."

She tells you that you are kind, and that she cannot come with you.

"But you're alone," you tell her. And then, with your own foundations crumbling, "*I'm* alone."

She asks you to leave. She asks you to leave like lovers ask each other to stay, like it's the greatest gift you could give her. You want to do whatever she tells you to, you really do. But she won't come with you, so you do the only logical thing: you stay. When she realizes this, she softly guides your eyelids closed, running a single finger over your eyelashes. "Pretty," she mumbles. You feel the brush of lips on your eyelid, then right below your eye, then on the sharpest angle of your cheekbone. She's checking your skin for solidity. She's making sure that underneath it all you're not bloating liquids and maggots. Sensible, you think. Without opening your eyes, you turn your head and catch her lips with yours. The letter in your pocket protests, begs you to keep moving; you deepen the kiss.

You stay as the floor crumbles to dust and the worms spread, and you stay as the foundation collapses underneath you, then buries you. There is pain, but there is contentment, however brief, in finding someone to care about again. And as you slip into nothingness, you hear the din of the towns-people, but above that you hear her solid voice, "Well done, darling. Thank you." The maggots burrow into you, "But you have a message," she reminds.

The pain disappears all at once. You are outside the town, covered in grime, alone. You lie there awhile. And when you stand, the slick mud under your feet tries to drag you back down. You are unsteady, again.

VI. THERE IS NOTHING HERE

The snow crunching beneath your sneakers disturbs the dead air. You're not at all dressed for this. It was—August?—when you started this journey. Wasn't it? You're pretty sure. Your feet should be prickling with cold in your soaked-through shoes. You should have frostbite, should be sinking into a numb sleep that you'd never wake up from, but you're fine. Or, that's not true, you're—miserable—yes, that's it. You didn't know it before now, but that's what this impossible weight is. You look behind to see if you can catch a glimpse of Mission far below, but your former home has hidden its destruction under a lurking fog. No, the snow won't be your death. That's not allowed.

As you glance around at the bleak, blinding landscape, it dawns on you: there is nothing here.

Surely not *nothing*, your rationale fights back.

No, no, you insist. There is nothing.

You look for something beyond the white expanse to prove yourself wrong—even in the winter, your mountain has evergreens and gray rock and rabbits and birds—but there is nothing.

Once, when you were barely eighteen, right when you were starting to realize that no amount of saving up was getting you to college, that you were going to stay in Mission until—well, it seems morbid now, but the thought you had then was, *I'll be here till hell swallows this place whole*—your Mama left town to go visit your granddad—your dad's dad—in Florida. It was January, and the night after she left, an ice storm hit. The day after that, a snowstorm. Then another ice storm, then a snowstorm. Your house was right on the edge of town, at the end of a long, dirt road behind the trailer park. The snowplows weren't going to get to you for days, maybe a week or more. You were plenty stocked up on food and firewood, so there were no worries there, and it started out fine enough. The first couple of days it was sort of fun—you were young, and even stuck in your home there's an appeal of being able to choose what you have for dinner every night, deciding what TV show you're going to watch when the lights go out. It was quiet, yes, but it often was in your home. Your Mama had always been a sedate sort of woman, always spoke like everything was a gentle secret just for you.

After a little while, the silence started to get to you. Snow dampens sound, you knew this, but it was almost uncanny. You should have at least been able to hear the children in the trailer park yelling. They should've made piles of snow by now that were just big enough to slide down on pieces of cardboard. Maybe kids don't do that anymore, you thought, with all of the confidence of an eighteen-year-old who fully believes themself to be an adult. Maybe it was colder than you realized and their parents were worried about frostbite.

The days stretched on, and you got into the habit of leaving the TV going, just to have a bit of background noise. You stepped out onto the porch or peeked out the window a couple times a day to check on the state of the world. You tried to squint through the reflective white to check on the trailer park, to see if you could see anyone outside. It was still.

On the fifth day, the TV shut off while you were eating a breakfast of buttered toast and canned pears. You got up to fix it, hit the side of the TV a couple times, then jostled it back into place. Nothing happened. Mama must've forgotten to pay the cable bill, you reasoned. Returning to the kitchen, you reached over to the old radio your Mama sometimes listened to while cooking and flicked it on. The air filled with static and you began shuffling through stations. No signal.

You turned the radio off, sat in silence for a minute, and then turned it back on. Static was better than nothing.

You wanted a cigarette. Your Mama didn't know you'd started smoking—or more likely, she knew but she hadn't brought it up yet. But you never smoked in the house and you didn't have any stashed.

During that time, your thoughts started to come apart from one another.

Small routines continued: you made yourself get up before noon, turn on the static, make breakfast, briefly step out onto the porch to peer out into the white expanse before the silence from down the road sank into your stomach. An idea, quick and irrational, kept pushing to the forefront of your thoughts: if you were to follow the road, you'd find nothing. You'd make it to the end, except there wouldn't be an end. There would be no trailer park, no children, no dogs barking, no town beyond. It would be an endless road that led to nothing, no matter how long you walked. You began to ration your food, though you never actually let yourself consciously think that you would run out.

It was so quiet. The static was maddening. You wanted a cigarette.

It chased you to your dreams: standing at the end of a long, gravel road in a white expanse where your town used to be, the itch of nicotine scraping the back of your throat.

It's a small memory in the end, as all your memories seem now. Nothing dire happened. Maybe you lost your mind a bit, but you came back to yourself, and the whole thing felt silly in retrospect, as breakdowns often do. The children in the trailer park still existed, the radio turned back on. The day after the snow plows came, you made the hour-long walk to the gas station to get your cigarettes. Maggie—gas station Maggie—was there, waiting behind the counter as always. By the time you got home you were too cold to smoke outside, and so you sat at the kitchen table, eyes closed, smoking and listening to your chirping little radio inform you of trivial local happenings. The helplessness washed away and the novelty of feeling like an adult settled back in. When your Mama came home, the first thing she said to you after a quiet greeting and a hug was a request to please not smoke at all but if you must, don't do it in the house.

Your footsteps sink deep into the snow. Sheets of wind cut across your cheek like layers of geology. It should be exhausting, but it's not. You're also not sure you're going up anymore. Most likely you are—where else would you be going?—but the world doesn't feel tilted. Every step is horizontal and shuffling, one after the other after the other, dragging into tedium. The mountain is a never-ending expanse.

You liked Maggie. You didn't know her, had barely ever spoken to her, but you liked her. "Morning," you said to her, every day. You passed her your credit card, she passed you your cigarettes.

"Morning," she mumbled. She wore the same gray sweatshirt every day. Her makeup always looked like it had been done three days ago and hadn't been freshened once.

There are no birds on the mountainside. Where are the birds? There should be a couple flitting around, even with the heavy snow. A robin, warm brown-red against the white, breaking the monotony, a reminder that spring will come. There should be a robin.

Maggie never changed in all the time you saw her. And while that should've made her seem like a prop in your life, it did the opposite. Nothing seemed more real to you than her unchanging self. She had a million lives in your mind, all of them as mundane and invariable as the next. Maggie lived in the trailer park right next to you, with a dog and a girlfriend, and it was a funny little coincidence that you had never seen her there before. Maggie worked all day at a gas station so she could go home and play the guitar in the evenings—the only thing she really enjoyed. Maggie had been married twice: the first ended tragically, the second with a slow drifting apart. Maggie had grown up in Waco, Texas, and moved here to take care of her elderly father, who had been in prison for most of her life. He died nine years ago, but she stuck around.

There are no squirrels or rabbits. You cannot see your breath. There's no variation in the snow. You're not falling into pockets of mole-dug earth, you're not bumping into fallen branches or other detritus. Your pace remains uninterrupted. You cannot see your breath. There is nothing here.

The only day you recall Maggie not being there when you walked through the gas station doors, the replacement attendant did not say "good morning" back. You wanted to ask where Maggie was, but you had a sudden and acute fear that they would tell you she had died. She was back the next day like she never left, sliding you your cigarettes and mumbling her good morning.

Your eyes scan upwards to see how much further you have to go, but it's impossible to tell. You want to check on the letter, pull it out of your jacket, reassure yourself of its presence, but you're too scared of losing it in the vast emptiness.

In all the lives you ever thought up for Maggie, there was never one where she wasn't lonely. There were some where she went home to a husband and children, ones where she had eight siblings and faithfully attended the United Methodist Church next to the courthouse every Sunday. But even in those realities, she was unendingly lonely.

Not fully lacking in self-awareness, you know that you projected those feelings onto Maggie, that you have no idea what kind of life she had outside of the two minutes you saw her every morning. You know that, in all likelihood, she was loved, just as you were loved.

You were loved, and you were lonely, and you were not alone in this phenomenon. Your home, your family, friends, elementary school, were taken by the earth, and you do not feel any more lonely than the day before they were all taken away. Which is to say, you feel like you will never hold someone's hand ever again.

Maggie didn't turn up for her shift at the gas station today. She's dead.

Your Mama—you wonder if she'd ever returned from her trip to Florida, or if you had been imagining her all these years. You weren't a bad child, but you must've been frustrating. Indifferent to school, apathetic to the idea of any specific career, too shy to properly pursue a partner. Annie had been brief, and you're pretty sure she asked you out. Hadn't she? You can't quite recall.

Once your Mama had asked you, "If you could do anything at all, what would you do?" And you shrugged, and said, "I guess I'd sit up on the hill behind the trailers and watch the town."

"Watch it do what? What's there to watch?" she had asked.

You shrugged again and said, "People."

It's possible, you suppose, that she'd never come back. That those two weeks alone in the snow had driven you to conjuring her presence in the house just so you wouldn't have to be by yourself. She was, come to think of it, always just real enough: her smile was always so practiced, her voice so even, soft—she was a southern belle robbed of fortune, wrapped in a faded housedress. If you had imagined up a Mama, you couldn't have threaded the needle better. Not that it matters now. She either never came back or she's dead.

Was it *me?* You wonder suddenly. Oh god, what if it was me? What if the resentment and fear and emptiness of sitting at the end of a dirt road all through your twenties, making dinner from cans and sitting and watching TV and going to work the next day, over and over and over again, hollowed the earth and swallowed everything whole, leaving only you alive to spread your poison elsewhere, until that place collapses, and you move on, forever.

Your town is gone and your Mama is gone and Annie is gone and Maggie is gone and Danny is gone and there is nothing here. There is nothing here but you are here which means you are nothing, or it means that you are something surrounded by nothing, which might be worse—to be this, forever—there has to be someone else—you scramble for the envelope, desperate to know it's still there. Your hands tremble as you shuffle around, trying to remember what pocket you put the letter in, but when you find it, it remains dry and safe. The wanting overcomes your fear of losing it—you pull the envelope out and hold it in your hands, wrinkling it in your haste to feel the slightly textured paper. It looks like nice paper. You hadn't noticed that before. You run a finger along the edge, feel the rise where the letter sits inside.

You should open it. It might be able to tell you something, give you a comforting message, ease the marrow-piercing lonely, but you can't. Every time you go to try, your body circumvents the action, some unknown instinct taking over. Nevertheless, you keep hold of the envelope, rubbing your calloused thumb across it, begging its presence to bring an end to the nothingness.

When you look back up, you see a cluster of pines not ten feet in the distance. The sight sends a wave of relief rushing through you, and you gently put the message back in your jacket. In the same way you have not been able to resist this momentum since beginning your climb, you move forward. The pines whisper. A light breeze moves through, leaves a cool touch on your cheek. A shuffling noise comes from past the trees, accompanied by a low sound like a breathy laugh. You move forward. The snow is less around the trees, a mere dusting among fallen needles, pillowing mosses, anemic lichen. A droplet of water falls from a branch and hits the back of your neck, cold and shocking. An insect buzzes past your ear. There is something, there is *something*.

A voice from beyond the pines, crackling and pitched: "I'm over here, darlin."

You step into the clearing and see first an impossible lake, stretching beyond your immediate vision, and second, a black vulture, crouched, neck craned out and looking back at you with intelligent dark eyes. Then the vulture straightens out in a slow, stiff motion that looks painful. It keeps standing straighter, and taller, and then all at once it's not a vulture but a man with a vulture's head perched atop his shoulders.

You take a moment to comprehend this, some previously unfelt fear building inside you, and then all at once you sink back into the calm.

VII. THE MAN WITH THE VULTURE HEAD

The man with the vulture head opens his hooked beak. Before he has a chance to talk, you raise a hand to stop him, fumble for the envelope, and hold it out. "I have a message," you say.

His fingers, long and thin and holding the appearance of having been dipped in black ink, twitch, but he doesn't take it from you. "So you do," he sighs.

"I'm—from Mission." It's the only thing you can think to say.

"I know this."

"I have a message," you repeat. These are two things you know: where you're from, and what you're here to do. This time you take a step forward, holding the envelope out more insistently.

The man with the vulture head hesitates, then reaches out. When he takes the message, he splits the envelope open casually with a tapered nail as if it is nothing. As if you did not carry it through choking kudzu and rotting landslides to get here. He splits it open as if it is not sacred.

For the first time since you watched your home sink into the earth and be gone, you feel anger and you are sure, in this moment, that you could crumble this mountain to dust on that anger alone. You raise a hand to snatch the letter back; *he doesn't deserve it*, a voice rumbles in your head. Your movement is cut short by a click from the vulture's beak, a hiss, and the words, "It's for you, darlin."

You frown, shake your head even as you take it back. The anger simmers down and lies in wait. You look down at the letter, now safely back in your hands.

"Go on, read it."

Surely not, you think. It can't be for you, or you would have opened it sooner. You wouldn't have needed to climb a goddamn mountain. You wouldn't have needed to give the everything of the nothing that you have in order to read it. But he stares, and you don't think he will stop until you do what he says, so you open it, and you read the message.

It doesn't make much sense. It hasn't told you why your home is gone, or why you had to climb a mountain to learn absolutely nothing. You read it again, because it has to mean something. It was not in your pocket, and then the earth ate your home, and then it was in your pocket, and then you dragged your grief-ridden body here to get some answers, so it must mean something. You look at the vulture. His eyes are unblinking and heavy and there is an emotion in them you cannot identify. "Are you fucking with me?" you ask.

He tilts his head to the side, slow. "You are tired," he says.

"I'm angry," you correct.

"Rapture and decay," he says.

"What?"

Like a sudden summer downpour, you are human again. Sensation re-entering your sleeping limbs spikes through you. You are cavernously starving. You are, as he said, so, so tired.

"I've saved you a spot," says the man with the vulture head. He nods to the space next to him, and then to the endless expanse of water behind him. For a moment you think he's asking you to die. You shake your head again. He would smile, if beaks could bare teeth. "All I ask for is a bit of company," he clarifies.

On trembling, exhausted legs, you move to take your place next to where he stands under a twisting pitch pine. He turns his gaze away from you towards the lake, and you follow his eyes. Now that you're looking properly, you think you can see the shore on the other side if you squint. The water laps up on the sand, swaying forward and back like a final waltz. A humidity rises, a little boggy, buggy, calm, but for ripples of fish and insects. "I didn't think I'd find it, to be honest."

"Find what, darlin'?"

"The end," you say. "I think—I think I believed I'd be walking forever. That I had become…" You can't finish the sentence. It sounds ridiculous, even now.

"My dear, this isn't the end."

"Oh," you breathe. "Why?"

What other question could you have?

The man with the vulture head laughs. It's a shrieking, gurgling thing. "You are *funny*," he says. And then, with care, he tells you this: that sometimes the weight is too much. "The earth is soft and erosion is inevitable. There is no fault to this. Just—fluctuation. Rise and fall. The steady breaths of the earth deep in its sleep."

"Rapture and decay," you say.

"Just so," he assents.

He goes on: The living must adjust with this fluctuation, and the dead needn't do anything about it. Survival is dependent on the ability to adjust. To live among and atop something as massive as the earth is to accept this and take loss as it is: excruciating and necessary. He goes on: the breathing will stop, eventually. Not for a while, not until most things that we recognize as life have returned to dust. The rise and fall will slow, the time between movements will stretch, and then it will stop, and be still.

He goes on: Have you ever tried to catch the exact day that fall transitions to winter? One day there are trees, full of vibrant leaves, the air is crisp, the breeze harkens towards winter. And then there are a few trees who have lost their leaves—you notice that, you do. But the precise moment of transition is too gradual to catch, and one day you awaken to find all the leaves are on the ground, damp and packed and on their way to becoming earth themselves, the trees are dark, skeletal silhouettes, the air bites, and you missed it again. The last leaf to fall did so in the pre-dawn blue light and went unnoticed by all. This is how the earth's last breath will occur; quiet, and in the blue light of the dawn of something else.

The man with the vulture head tells you that he will be there at the end, and for the something else that will come after.

"That sounds lonely," you say.

He dips his beak in acknowledgment, admits that many fates are.

He goes on. There is much to do before the final breath. Intervention is not intrusion. Collapse is the land crying for help, and shifting dirt should be brought to balance. The earth, despite its magnitude, does not exist unbroken. There are things that would bring about the final breath before its time. There is responsibility in our movement. Breath comes with the duty to help others breathe.

The man with the vulture head slumps to the side, catches himself on the pine's trunk. You reach out to help, but he shakes his head in a slow, swaying motion, beak and shoulders dipping low, his body a sail with no wind to keep it going.

He continues, gasping now. He tells you that you still breathe. There are many who do not, but you are not one of them, not yet.

You can't help it; you ask what's happening to him. You've read the letter so you already know, but he is gracious enough to explain again. He points to you: "Rise," he says. Points to himself, "and fall. Rapture," he gestures for you to complete the phrase.

"And decay," you say.

He nods. "Are you going to ask why it has to be you? That's what I wanted to know when I was chosen."

You shrug. "I figured the answer to that would be something like *why is anyone chosen?* or something equally cryptic, to be honest."

He laughs again, that strange clicking noise, which turns into a long, slow sigh. "You'll be just fine, darlin."

"I do have one question."

"Of course."

"You said it will be you, at the end, but you're—so—will it be me?"

The man with the vulture head hums. "It will be you in the same way it will be me. This task—to balance and watch—is an inheritance, so it could be the you that you are now, or it could be the you who embraces you, yes?"

To your own bafflement, your head settles into this explanation as if it makes any sense at all.

"Will you help me get to the water?" he asks.

You nod, heft him up, and walk him over to the edge of the shoreline. He sinks to the ground and you descend with him. When he leans over the shifting waters, you lean with him. His face clarifies first, dark reflection sharp on the silvery surface. As your eyes drift over to your own reflection, you blink, bow closer. For one strange moment, you don't recognize what looks back—you're not—are you?—no, this is you. The one with the coyote head. It takes a brief moment of wondering—were you always?—surely you must have been. You have always had tawny fur and scavenging eyes. You have always had teeth destined for rending. Of course. Of course you have. You push away the unease. It's you, the one with the coyote head. Hello.

Next to you, the reflection of the man with the vulture head shifts, and you pull your eyes away from your own image to turn to him. His chest moves slower and heavier with each inhale, almost as if he's sleeping, but his eyes are open and aware.

"It's almost your time," he says. "Are you ready?"

You suppose that you are. You turn back to the water.

His change happens in silence. You glimpse it out of the corner of your eyes: he stretches, straightens his back, spreads his arms—no, wings—black and glinting. Sunlight peeks through his flight feathers, divine, grasping. The man with the vulture head becomes only a vulture, then he sinks low. It occurs to you that watching this transformation through the water may be an unbearable act of cowardice, and you turn away from the lake, lean forward, envelop him, and sigh into his hollow bones. His feathers are warm, like cotton t-shirts drying on the line on a sunny day. Wings tucked into body, body curled loose around itself, as if in a deep, comfortable sleep, but there is no breath.

You sit up and run your hand along the dead bird's spine, just once. It falls into decomposition in tandem with the movement—flesh sinks, becomes dirt, feeds worms. The merging hurts, but only for a moment. Then you blink and look down into the lake again. It is you, the one with the coyote head, but your eyes are new.

Hello, the vulture says.

"Hi," you whisper.

Now how does that feel, darlin?

It's all very familiar. You close your eyes, feel the lake's breeze play with your fur. Your ear twitches. Your fingers are pleasantly cold.

Darlin?

Ah, right there. You can hear it now. "Mama?"

A bit, the vulture admits.

"The others?"

A bit.

You cross your legs and lean back. "You'll stay?"

Of course.

The mountain moves beneath you. You can feel it now, the constant shift. Your weight, balancing it out. It will not fall yet. Vision set towards the water in front of you, ears trained towards the clearing behind you, you sit, and you watch, and you wait.

ACKNOWLEDGMENTS

Firstly and always, thanks to those who sustain me in love and keep me feeling excited to make new art. The list is long, and I will name only a few: Sam, Jordan, Laura, Ash, and Cortni, thank you.

Thank you to the dirt and trees and moss and animals of Spruce Knob in West Virginia, particularly the cheerfully loud Barred Owl who refused to let me sleep at night. Thank you to the creatures and green things and dirt of Kentucky, including but certainly not limited to: Red River Gorge, Happy Top, the preserve at Shaker Village, and my homedirt. The best writing in this book is thanks to you.

Endless gratitude to the dedicated and enthusiastic team at Split Lip Press. Kate and Kristine, for cleaning up my manuscript and making it shine, David, for the most incredible cover, and Gage and Abby, who make the deep, dark cave of marketing a less mysterious place.

Thank you to Jay and Donna (and the garden, Moxa, Dora, and Diego) at Wormfarm Institute, who gave me a space to write the final edits of this book, as well as my fellow artist residents there, whose insightful conversations roll around in my head with every word I write.

Thank you Mama, for teaching me to write real good and for bringing me back home. Thank you Dad, for our times in the woods and water. It's possible neither of you may ever read this, but I'm grateful anyhow.

Lastly, to the myriad folks of various hollers and fields who have taught me many ways of being:

to everyone I've ever shared a dance with,
cooked a meal with,
worked a garden with,
built a fire with,
ever taught a song to,
ever learnt a song from,
thank you.

EM J PARSLEY (also known as Wylde) is a poet, novelist, environmentalist, and gardener who usually lives in rural Kentucky. He is the author of the poetry chapbook, *the anonym gospels* (April Gloaming Publishing, 2024) which won the Apogee Poetry Chapbook Award. This is their first novella.

NOW AVAILABLE FROM SPLIT/LIP PRESS

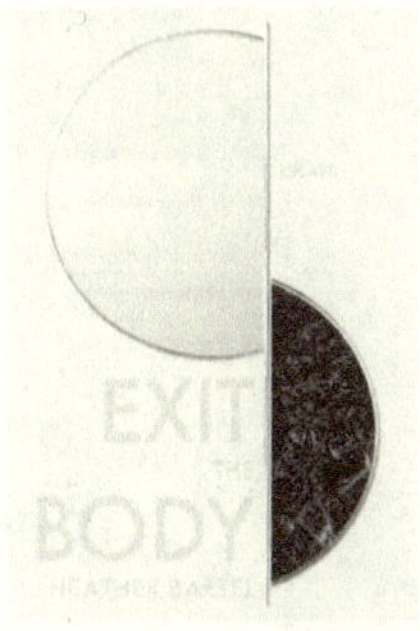

For more info about the press and titles,
visit us at www.splitlippress.com

Follow us on Instagram and Twitter: @splitlippress

www.ingramcontent.com/pod-product-compliance
Lightning Source LLC
LaVergne TN
LVHW051021080826
845145LV00009B/2738